Pebble® Plus

Let's Look at Light

How Are Shadows and Reflections Made?

by Mari Schuh

PEBBLE
a capstone imprint

Pebble Plus is published by Pebble
1710 Roe Crest Drive, North Mankato, Minnesota 56003
www.mycapstone.com

Library of Congress Cataloging-in-Publication Data
Names: Schuh, Mari C., 1975- author.
Title: How are shadows and reflections made? / by Mari Schuh.
Description: North Mankato, Minnesota : Pebble, a Capstone imprint, [2020] |
   Series: Pebble plus. Let's look at light | Audience: Ages 4-8. | Includes
   bibliographical references and index.
Identifiers: LCCN 2018060250| ISBN 9781977108944 (hardcover) | ISBN
   9781977110411 (pbk.) | ISBN 9781977108982 (ebook pdf)
Subjects: LCSH: Light--Properties--Juvenile literature. | Shades and
   shadows--Juvenile literature. | Reflection (Optics)--Juvenile literature.
Classification: LCC QC360 .S3785 2020 | DDC 535.2--dc23
LC record available at https://lccn.loc.gov/2018060250

Editorial Credits

Karen Aleo, editor; Kyle Grenz, designer; Tracy Cummins, media researcher; Laura Manthe, production specialist

Photo Credits

Alamy: Myrleen Pearson, 21; iStockphoto: DeborahMaxemow, 11, Yuri_Arcurs, 19; Science Source: Julie Dermansky, 13; Shutterstock: akachai studio, 9, Andrew S, Cover Bottom, biletskiy, 7, Julia Kuznetsova, 17, m.rudziewicz, Cover Top, Mercury Green, 15, Patrick Tr, 1, Tabby Mittins, Cover Back, wavebreakmedia, 5

Note to Parents and Teachers

The Let's Look at Light set supports national standards related to light and energy. This book describes and illustrates shadows and reflections. The images support early readers in understanding the text. The repetition of words and phrases helps early readers learn new words. This book also introduces early readers to subject-specific vocabulary words, which are defined in the Glossary section. Early readers may need assistance to read some words and to use the Table of Contents, Glossary, Read More, Internet Sites, Critical Thinking, and Index sections of the book.

All internet sites appearing in back matter were available and accurate when this book was sent to press.

Table of Contents

Rays of Light

Light helps us see. It moves
in straight lines called rays.
Rays of light travel quickly.
They keep moving until
they hit an object.

Look at the rainbow!
Sunlight shines through
water droplets. The water
bends the rays of light.
Colors in the rays separate.

Shadows and Light

Look at the shadow on the ground. It moves when the girl moves. Shadows are made when light is blocked.

Many objects block light.

These objects are opaque.

A shadow forms behind

the object.

Less light can get there.

Shadows can be

different sizes.

The cat is close to the light.

So it blocks lots of light.

The cat's shadow is big.

Light Passes Through Objects

Translucent objects let some light pass through them. You can't clearly see through them. Objects on the other side look fuzzy.

Transparent objects let all light pass through them. Clean windows are transparent. You can see through them!

Reflecting Light

When light reflects,

it bounces off objects.

Then you can see them.

Shiny metal objects reflect

lots of light.

Mirrors reflect the light that
hits them. Light rays
bounce back to you.
So you can see yourself!
What else reflects light?

Glossary

opaque—not see-through; blocking all rays of light

ray—a line of light that beams out from something bright

reflect—to return light from an object

shadow—the dark shape made when something blocks light

sunlight—light that comes from the sun

translucent—partly see-through; letting some rays of light to pass through

transparent—clear and easily seen through; letting all rays of light to pass through

Read More

Best, B. J. *Reflectiveness of Light.* Properties of Matter. New York: Cavendish Square, 2019.

James, Emily. *The Simple Science of Light.* Simply Science. North Mankato, Minn.: Capstone, 2018.

Royston, Angela. *All About Light.* All About Science. Chicago: Heinemann Raintree, 2016.

Internet Sites

Easy Science for Kids: Shadows
https://easyscienceforkids.com/shadows/

Looking in the Mirror Coloring Page
http://www.supercoloring.com/coloring-pages/looking-in-the-mirror

Super-cool stuff! Check out projects, games, and lots more at **www.capstonekids.com**

Critical Thinking Questions

1. How are shadows made?
2. Describe opaque objects and transparent objects.
3. Name two kinds of objects that reflect lots of light.

Index